Flatfoot Fox

and the Case of the Missing Schoolhouse

Flatfoot Fox

and the Case of the Missing Schoolhouse

ETH CLIFFORD

Illustrated by Brian Lies

Houghton Mifflin Company

Boston 1997

In loving memory of a dear friend,
Nathaniel Rosenberg
— E.C.

For Mame
— B.L.

For information about this and other Houghton Mifflin trade
and reference books and multimedia products, visit
The Bookstore at Houghton Mifflin on the World Wide Web
at http://www.hmco.com/trade/.

Library of Congress Cataloging-in-Publication Data

Clifford, Eth,
     Flatfoot Fox and the case of the missing schoolhouse / Eth
Clifford : illustrated by Brian Lies.
          p.   cm.
     Summary: Flatfoot Fox and his faithful friend, Secretary Bird,
help Principal Porcupine solve the mystery of the missing school.
     ISBN 0-395-81446-4
     [1. Foxes—Fiction.   2. Animals—Fiction.   3. Mystery and
detective stories.]   I. Lies, Brian, ill.   II. Title.
PZ7.C62214Fm   1997
[Fic]—dc20   96-11665
                         CIP
                         AC

Manufactured in the United States of America
The text of this book is set in 14 pt. Century Schoolbook
BP   10   9   8   7   6   5   4   3   2   1

Contents

1. A New Kind of Mystery   7

2. The Schoolhouse Went . . . Whsssssssh! 15

3. Magicians, Magicians, Everywhere 23

4. The Dee-Double-Dare 31

5. A Sensible Question 41

6. How Long Is a Little While? 47

1.
A New Kind of Mystery

Knock! Knock! Knock!

Flatfoot Fox hurried to open the door. Secretary Bird was asleep and Flatfoot Fox didn't want the knocking to wake him up.

The visitor walked in and said, "We need you."

"Of course you do," Flatfoot Fox agreed at once. "Everybody does."

Just then Secretary Bird woke up. He stared at the stranger.

"Who are you?" he wanted to know.

"I am Principal Porcupine," the stranger began, "and I . . ."

Secretary Bird interrupted. "Don't tell me. Let me guess. Something is missing, and you want us to find out where it is and who took it."

"Us?" Principal Porcupine was surprised. "Are you a detective, too?"

Secretary Bird looked at Flatfoot Fox. Flatfoot Fox looked at Secretary Bird.

"Well, no. Not exactly. But I do help," Secretary Bird said. "I help a lot."

Flatfoot Fox smiled. "Of course you do," he told Secretary Bird. Then he asked Principal Porcupine, "Is something missing?"

"Oh yes," Principal Porcupine said. He was silent for a moment. Then he went on, "I don't know how to tell you this, because you won't believe me. I can't believe it myself!"

"I love mysteries I can't believe." Secretary Bird was delighted.

"Tell me," Flatfoot Fox said. "I will believe you."

"No matter how impossible it sounds?"

"No matter," Flatfoot Fox told him. "I will believe you."

"It's the schoolhouse . . ."

"Aha!" Secretary Bird cried. "One of your students is stealing some . . ."

"No, no, no," Flatfoot Fox said. "That's not it at all. This is something much more serious, isn't it?"

"It's the schoolhouse," Principal Porcupine said again. He began to weep. "Our brand-new schoolhouse is missing!"

"The schoolhouse?" Secretary Bird shook his head. "That's ridiculous. That's the most ridiculous thing I've ever heard. How can a schoolhouse be missing?"

"I don't know. That's why I need the smartest detective in the whole world."

Secretary Bird opened his mouth to say something, but closed it again when Flatfoot Fox shook his head.

"I couldn't believe it myself," Principal Porcupine agreed. "But it's true. The schoolhouse is gone. When I went there this morning, it was missing. Gone. Vanished. Disappeared. Out of sight. Nowhere . . ." He stopped to dry his tears.

Before he could speak again, Secretary Bird said, "Just leave it to us . . . to Flatfoot Fox. He will go with you, find suspects, ask them questions and look for clues. Then he will solve the mystery."

Flatfoot Fox shook his head. "Not this time," he said. "This is different. I think Principal Porcupine knows who stole the missing schoolhouse."

Principal Porcupine stared at Flatfoot Fox. "You *are* the smartest detective in the whole world. You are right. I do know who the thief is."

"No, No, NO! That is not the way to solve a mystery," Secretary Bird said. "Who ever heard of such a thing?"

"Hmmmm," Flatfoot Fox said. "What we have here is not a 'who-did-it?' mystery but a 'how-was-it-done?' mystery. Very interesting."

Secretary Bird was excited. "Then tell us! Tell us who did it. Who stole the schoolhouse?"

"Why it was Wacky Weasel, of course," Principal Porcupine said.

Flatfoot Fox nodded. "Because he told you he was going to do it. He probably even boasted about it."

"Oh, he boasted about it all right. He boasted and laughed."

"But why?" Secretary Bird asked. "Who is this Wacky Weasel? Why would he do such a thing?"

"He's one of my neighbors. And he did this to teach me a lesson."

"He wants to teach a *principal* a lesson?"

"Yes. Because he told me he is a magician. And I laughed at him. He's never done one magic trick right. All my neighbors laughed at him, too. So he told me he would get even. He said he would make the schoolhouse disappear. And he did it. He really did it. The schoolhouse *is* missing. And school opens in two weeks."

"Then let's go find it," said Flatfoot Fox. "There is no time to lose."

"It's way out in the country," Principal Porcupine said. "It will take us a while to get there."

He raced out the door. Flatfoot Fox followed.

"Wait," Secretary Bird said. "We'll need an umbrella. It always rains in the country."

He grabbed the umbrella, which flew open. A strong wind lifted Secretary Bird into the air.

Principal Porcupine asked, "Is he always in such a hurry to solve a mystery?"

Flatfoot Fox laughed. "I think it may take a while, no matter how fast the wind carries him."

2.
The Schoolhouse Went . . . Whsssssssh!

"Are we almost there?" Secretary Bird asked.

The wind was just a gentle breeze now, so Secretary Bird had closed the umbrella. He had landed on the path right behind Flatfoot Fox and Principal Porcupine.

"Oh yes. We're almost there. We should be seeing a sign soon," Principal Porcupine explained. "See? Here it is."

"Why did you put up a sign?" Secretary Bird asked. "Don't you know how to get to the schoolhouse?"

"Of course I do. That sign is up there for anyone who is a stranger and doesn't know how to get to the schoolhouse. I look at it anyway. It makes me feel good."

The sign was on a tree. It pointed to a lane between a row of trees. It said: TO THE OLD COUNTRY SCHOOLHOUSE.

"Why does it say 'Old Country Schoolhouse' if the schoolhouse is new?" Secretary Bird wondered.

"It's called that because this was once called Old Country Lane. I liked the sound of it, so I used that name for our schoolhouse," Principal Porcupine explained.

"Why is the sign crooked?" Flatfoot Fox wondered.

"The wind, I guess," Principal Porcupine told him.

Flatfoot Fox looked very thoughtful as he stared up at the sign. He began to ask another question, but just then they heard a voice calling.

"Oh dear," Principal Porcupine said. "I should have known he would turn up."

"Who's turned up?" asked Secretary Bird.

Principal Porcupine waved his paw. "That's one of my neighbors, Believable Badger. He thinks he's a magician, too."

16

He ran down the lane, with Flatfoot Fox and Secretary Bird right behind him. He stopped suddenly and paid no attention to Believable Badger. "Look!" he said and pointed. "This is what I wanted to show you."

"Look at what?" Secretary Bird said. "All I see is just a lot of land with nothing on it."

"Exactly." Principal Porcupine agreed.

"Yes, but . . ." Believable Badger began, then stopped when Flatfoot Fox said, "Of course it's just a lot of land, with nothing on it . . . *now*. But that's just where the Old Country Schoolhouse was, before it disappeared."

"You're absolutely right," Principal Porcupine sighed. He dabbed his eyes with a handkerchief. "My beautiful schoolhouse — gone!"

"Yes, but . . ." Believable Badger tried again. He got no further because a voice behind them said, "Look at that! Ha! Ha! Ha! No schoolhouse!"

"Who are you?" Secretary Bird asked.

"That's Wacky Weasel. Don't talk to him," Principal Porcupine ordered. He turned and shouted at Wacky Weasel. "You said you would do it, and now you've gone and done it, and I just hope you're satisfied."

Wacky Weasel grinned. "Yes I did. I did it all right. I sure made that schoolhouse go . . . whsssssssh!"

"You did not!" Believable Badger shouted. "Believe me," he told Principal Porcupine, "I did it.

18

I was the one who made the schoolhouse go whsssssssh!"

Wacky Weasel laughed and laughed. "Look who thinks he's a magician," he said. "I bet you think you can make the sun come up in the morning."

"Don't tease him," Principal Porcupine said.

"I am so a magician!" Believable Badger insisted. "The schoolhouse is gone, isn't it? Well, I made it disappear and I can bring it back if I want to, believe me."

19

Principal Porcupine shook his head. "You know you can't. You know Wacky Weasel stole the schoolhouse."

Secretary Bird had been thinking. Now he turned to Wacky Weasel and Believable Badger and scolded them. "The very idea. Stealing something and then bragging about it. You ought to be ashamed . . ."

"Stealing?" Believable Badger was upset. "Doing magic isn't stealing!"

"I'm not a thief," Wacky Weasel was angry. "I do magic. Don't you even know the difference?"

He turned and stared at Flatfoot Fox. "Do you think I stole the schoolhouse?"

"No," said Flatfoot Fox.

Wacky Weasel grinned. "You'd like to solve this puzzle, wouldn't you?" he said. "They call you the smartest detective in the whole world. Well, this is one puzzle you will never solve."

Secretary Bird stared at Flatfoot Fox.

Was it true?

Was this a case that even the smartest detective
in the whole world would not be able to solve?

3.

Magicians,
Magicians, Everywhere

Flatfoot Fox didn't answer. He turned his head and listened. Everyone else listened, too.

"Oh dear," Principal Porcupine sighed. "Not them, too."

"Who's them?" Secretary Bird asked.

"Two more of my neighbors." He sighed again. "Smelly Skunk and Daffy Armadillo." He shouted at Wacky Weasel, "Ever since you boasted about being a magician, everybody else decided to become magicians, too. Go *home*," he snapped as Smelly Skunk and Daffy Armadillo came into view.

"I've come to make the schoolhouse reappear," Smelly Skunk said.

"We don't need you, believe me," Believable Badger shouted. "I'm the only real magician here. I made the schoolhouse disappear and . . ."

"No, you didn't," said Smelly Skunk. "The only thing you can make disappear is food. I'm the real magician. I'm the one who made the schoolhouse vanish."

Secretary Bird shook his head. What would Flatfoot Fox do now, with so many suspects? He pushed closer to Believable Badger and Smelly Skunk.

The minute he moved, Daffy Armadillo cried out, "Did you see that? Did you all see that? That tree just moved."

Secretary Bird turned his head and looked back. He didn't see a tree move. Leaves moved in the wind. Branches moved in the wind. But *trees?*

He walked a little closer.

"Stand back!" Daffy Armadillo yelled. "The tree is moving again."

Secretary Bird stared at Daffy Armadillo. "Whatever are you saying?" he asked.

"Help! Run for your lives!" Daffy Armadillo

sobbed. "That tree walked. And now it's talking. I don't like trees that walk and talk. Make it stop," he begged.

"Oh, do be quiet," Principal Porcupine snapped. He explained to Secretary Bird, "He doesn't see very well. And he doesn't hear very well, either."

"Silly thing," Secretary Bird grumbled. "Doesn't he know that trees can't walk . . . ?"

Flatfoot Fox laughed. Then he told Secretary Bird, "He thinks your long legs are skinny tree trunks."

"I don't care what he thinks," Secretary Bird answered. "Everybody knows trees can't walk."

"What's that the tree just said?" Daffy Armadillo asked. "Did it say that bees eat chalk? I didn't know that. What is this world coming to, with trees that talk and bees that eat chalk?"

"Be quiet," Smelly Skunk snapped at him. Then

26

he turned to Principal Porcupine. "Let's just get it
clear about who did what. Never mind what the
others say. I'm the only real magician around here.
I made the schoolhouse disappear. And only I can
make it reappear."

"That's ridiculous," Wacky Weasel snapped.

"Why doesn't anybody listen?" Believable Badger complained. "I'm the magician, believe me."

"No! I am!" the others shouted, even Daffy Armadillo, who didn't know why they were shouting.

27

"QUIET!" Principal Porcupine roared. "What is wrong with all of you? You know and I know that it was Wacky Weasel who made the schoolhouse disappear. And now Flatfoot Fox has come to find out how he did it and make him put the schoolhouse back where it belongs."

"I would have made the schoolhouse disappear," Daffy Armadillo whispered, "but I couldn't see it."

"You make me laugh," said Secretary Bird.

"A giraffe? Where?" Daffy Armadillo shook with fright. "Run, everybody! The giraffes are coming! The giraffes are coming!"

No one paid any attention to him.

Wacky Weasel moved closer to Flatfoot Fox. "Being the smartest detective in the world won't help you on this case. Only a magician can solve it," he laughed.

Flatfoot Fox stared at Wacky Weasel. "Maybe I am both," he said.

4.
The Dee-Double-Dare

Principal Porcupine was very angry. "You can't talk like that to Flatfoot Fox. You . . ."

"Yes I can," Wacky Weasel interrupted. "Everyone talks about how smart Flatfoot Fox is. Well, now he has met someone smarter than he is. I dare you to find out how I made the schoolhouse disappear. I dare you to make it reappear. I dee-double-dare you!"

Everyone stared at Wacky Weasel.

Everyone was speechless.

Secretary Bird was very worried. Was it possible for Wacky Weasel to be smarter than Flatfoot Fox? If it was up to him, he would advise Flatfoot Fox to leave. That was it! They ought to leave, right this very minute.

But Flatfoot Fox didn't look as if he wanted to leave. He just smiled. Then he said, "I accept your challenge."

Principal Porcupine sighed with relief.

"This is ridiculous. And it's not fair," Believable Badger said suddenly. "Why do you believe Wacky Weasel, anyway? I'm the best magician here, I should have first chance at making the schoolhouse reappear."

"No, no, no," Smelly Skunk called out. "I should go first. I know all the right magic words."

"Tragic birds?" Daffy Armadillo began to cry. "Something awful has happened to our birds?" He cried even harder. "It's his fault." He pointed in the general direction where he thought Secretary Bird was standing. "I knew something terrible would happen as soon as that tree started to walk and talk."

"Be quiet, all of you," Principal Porcupine ordered. "How can Flatfoot Fox think with all this noise? And stop your weeping," he told Daffy Armadillo.

32

"I am not sleeping," Daffy Armadillo told him. "How can anyone sleep . . ."

"It's all right," Flatfoot Fox said quickly. "Why don't we let them try to solve this puzzle, since they are so anxious to do so?"

Secretary Bird couldn't believe Flatfoot Fox said that.

Wacky Weasel laughed and laughed.

Believable Badger looked happy. "I'll go first because it was my idea," he said. He took a deep breath. He turned his head left. He turned his head right. Then he shook his head very, very hard. He

hummed a little tune softly. Then he hummed it louder and louder. At last he said, "Fee, fi, fo, fum . . ."

"Those aren't magic words," Smelly Skunk said.

"They're not?" Believable Badger asked. "It's all this talking — yakety-yakety — that made me forget. I'll start over again. Pease-porridge-hot, pease-porridge-cold . . . no, no, wait a minute. It will come to me. I have it! Hey-diddle-diddle, the cat and the fiddle, the cow jumped over the moon . . ."

"STOP!" Principal Porcupine roared. "I've heard enough."

"So have I," said Smelly Skunk.

"It's not fair. He's made me forget the real magic words," Believable Badger complained.

Smelly Skunk pushed him aside. "Now," he said, "here are the really real magic words. Just keep your eyes on the clearing. You'll see the schoolhouse reappear."

Everyone turned to stare at the empty field.

Smelly Skunk squeezed his eyes shut. Then he

said, in a singsong voice, "Abracadabra. Hocus-pocus, dominocus. SCHOOLHOUSE APPEAR!"

He kept his eyes closed, waiting for the happy shouts of the others when the schoolhouse reappeared. But everyone was silent.

Smelly Skunk opened his eyes.

"I don't understand," he said. "Those words are in my magic book. They're supposed to work every time. You know what I think?" Smelly Skunk was very angry. "I bet there never was a schoolhouse here! What do you think of that?"

"Sour grapes!" Wacky Weasel shouted. "Sour grapes!" He fell to the ground and pounded it while he laughed and laughed.

Principal Porcupine was furious.

"I've had enough of this. Now you will all be quiet while Flatfoot Fox finds the schoolhouse for us."

Wacky Weasel stood up and stared at Flatfoot Fox.

"I dee-double-dare you," he whispered.

Flatfoot Fox just smiled.

36

When Secretary Bird saw that smile, he felt good. He didn't know how, but he knew for sure that Flatfoot Fox had already solved the mystery.

But Principal Porcupine was upset. "How can you smile at a time like this? Can't you see that Wacky Weasel has really proved he is a magician?"

"Oh, yes," Flatfoot Fox answered. "He makes you believe that something has happened that hasn't happened at all, like any good magician. But you see, Smelly Skunk is right. The schoolhouse hasn't really disappeared."

Secretary Bird worried about Flatfoot Fox. Couldn't he see — couldn't they all see — that there was no schoolhouse in the field? He mentioned that softly to Flatfoot Fox, who said, "But there never *was* a schoolhouse here."

"What did I tell you?" Smelly Skunk shouted.

"Never was? That's unbelievable!" Believable Badger cried.

Daffy Armadillo was yawning so hard he didn't understand a word that was said.

Principal Porcupine shook his head. "How do you know the schoolhouse was never here?"

"Because of the sign," Flatfoot Fox told him. "Remember my telling you the sign was crooked? That sign will solve our mystery."

5.
A Sensible Question

Flatfoot Fox stood very still for a moment. Then he nodded, turned away, and began to race back along the lane.

"Aha!" said Wacky Weasel. "I knew he was a fake. He's running home."

"He didn't know any magic words, that's why," said Smelly Skunk. "That's why he's just run . . ."

"Won? Won what?" asked Daffy Armadillo.

"Flatfoot Fox hasn't run off," Secretary Bird said. "Flatfoot Fox . . ."

"Bats shoot rocks?" Daffy Armadillo interrupted. "Things are really strange around here today."

No one answered because they had all chased after Flatfoot Fox to see where he was going. When

Daffy called out and no one answered, he did what any sensible armadillo would do. He rolled up in a tight ball and fell asleep.

When all the others caught up with Flatfoot Fox, he was standing under the sign that said TO THE OLD COUNTRY SCHOOLHOUSE. Then he did a surprising thing. He asked Secretary Bird to reach up and remove the sign.

"Don't do that," Principal Porcupine said. "No one will know the way to the schoolhouse without that sign."

"He's right," Wacky Weasel said. "You put that sign right back this minute." He sounded worried.

Flatfoot Fox paid no attention. Instead he moved away swiftly. Secretary Bird hurried after him, still holding the sign. The others were not far behind. Flatfoot Fox raced past one lane and then another, looking up quickly each time. Then, at the next lane, he stopped and looked up at one of the trees.

"Of course," he said. He turned to Secretary Bird.

"Do you see a little knob on the branch, just above that scraped area?"

Secretary Bird looked up, then nodded.

"Hang the sign on it," Flatfoot Fox said.

"It looks just right hanging there," Secretary Bird said when the sign was in place.

"Of course it does. Because that's where it was to begin with. Follow me," he told them.

"I don't understand," Principal Porcupine complained. But Flatfoot Fox didn't hear him, because he had already begun to run along this new lane.

The others ran after him, then stopped suddenly. There, just in front of them, was the missing schoolhouse!

"Liar! Cheat! Faker!" Principal Porcupine shouted at Wacky Weasel, who had begun to sneak away.

Everyone else stared at Flatfoot Fox with their mouths open.

"You knew! You knew all the time," Secretary Bird said.

"Of course I knew," said Flatfoot Fox. "Because I asked myself a sensible question. *What do you do, I wondered, if you really can't move a schoolhouse? The answer was simple. *You don't move the schoolhouse. You just move the sign!*"

6.
How Long Is a Little While?

"It's good to be home again," Secretary Bird said.

"It's always good to be home," Flatfoot Fox agreed.

"Thinking this hard always makes me sleepy." Secretary Bird yawned. "It's especially hard when you have to find out not who did it but how it was done." Secretary Bird yawned again. "It just wears me out."

"Of course it does," Flatfoot Fox agreed again. "Why don't you rest your brain and take a little nap?"

"I'll do that right now. But I want you to promise me one thing. Promise you won't take on any more new cases for a while."

"I promise. But of course that depends on how long a little while is, doesn't it?"

Secretary Bird didn't answer.

He was sound asleep.

Flatfoot Fox leaned back in his chair. But he was wide awake, because he knew that, sooner or later, someone would be knocking on the door again.